Dear Parents:

Congratulations! Your child is taking the first steps on an exciting journey. The destination? Independent reading!

STEP INTO READING® will help your child get there. The program offers five steps to reading success. Each step includes fun stories and colorful art or photographs. In addition to original fiction and books with favorite characters, there are Step into Reading Non-Fiction Readers, Phonics Readers and Boxed Sets, Sticker Readers, and Comic Readers—a complete literacy program with something to interest every child.

Learning to Read, Step by Step!

Ready to Read   Preschool–Kindergarten
• big type and easy words • rhyme and rhythm • picture clues
For children who know the alphabet and are eager to begin reading.

Reading with Help   Preschool–Grade 1
• basic vocabulary • short sentences • simple stories
For children who recognize familiar words and sound out new words with help.

Reading on Your Own   Grades 1–3
• engaging characters • easy-to-follow plots • popular topics
For children who are ready to read on their own.

Reading Paragraphs   Grades 2–3
• challenging vocabulary • short paragraphs • exciting stories
For newly independent readers who read simple sentences with confidence.

Ready for Chapters   Grades 2–4
• chapters • longer paragraphs • full-color art
For children who want to take the plunge into chapter books but still like colorful pictures.

STEP INTO READING® is designed to give every child a successful reading experience. The grade levels are only guides; children will progress through the steps at their own speed, developing confidence in their reading.

Remember, a lifetime love of reading starts with a single step!

Step into Reading, Random House, and the Random House colophon are registered trademarks of Penguin Random House LLC.

Visit us on the Web!
StepIntoReading.com
randomhousekids.com

Educators and librarians, for a variety of teaching tools, visit us at RHTeachersLibrarians.com

ISBN 978-1-5247-0173-4 (trade) — ISBN 978-1-5247-0174-1 (lib. bdg.)

Printed in the United States of America   10 9 8 7 6 5 4 3 2 1

nickelodeon

TEENAGE MUTANT
NINJA TURTLES
OUT OF THE SHADOWS

MEAN TEAM

adapted by Geof Smith
illustrated by Patrick Spaziante

based on the screenplay "Teenage Mutant Ninja Turtles: Out of the Shadows"
by Josh Appelbaum and André Nemec

Random House 🏠 New York

Rocksteady is
a mutant rhino.
They are a mean team.

Bebop and Rocksteady
are on a plane.
They guard a crate.

A powerful alien device is in the crate. They will use it for evil.

The bad guys' plane
zooms through
the sky.

Another plane
follows them.
Who is on it?

The Turtles
leap from the plane!

Mikey rides

a rocket-propelled

skateboard!

The Turtles battle the bad guys inside the plane.

Donnie opens the crate.
The Turtles want
the alien device!

Splash!

The plane lands
in a river.

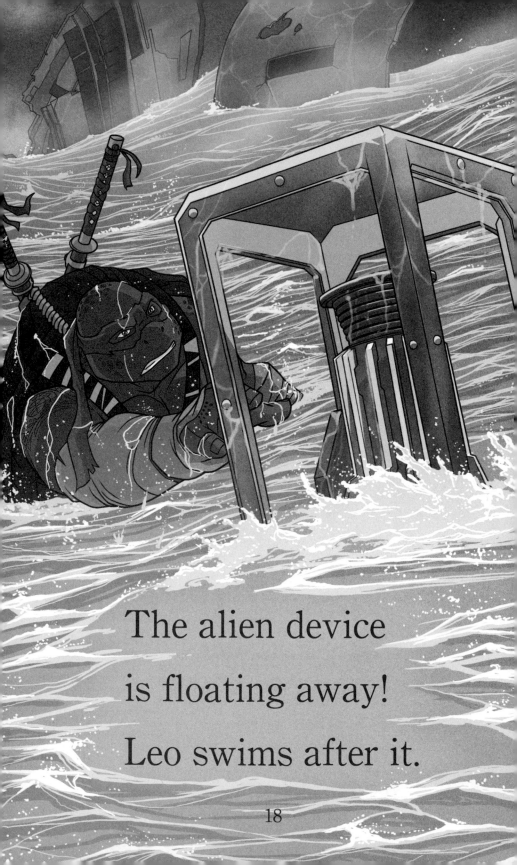

The alien device
is floating away!
Leo swims after it.

Rocksteady grabs
the alien device!

Bebop and Rocksteady
climb out of the river.
They have the device.

They escape from
the Turtles.

The Turtles tumble
over a waterfall!

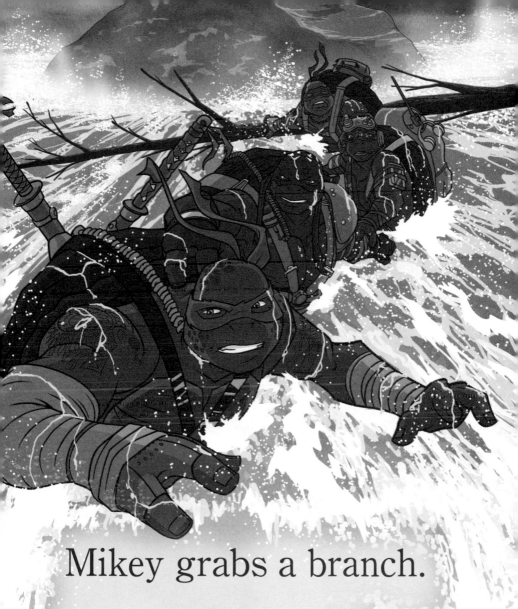

Mikey grabs a branch.

His brothers

hold on to him.

The Turtles are safe!

The Turtles will battle Bebop and Rocksteady another day!